We hope you enjoy this
Please return or renew it by the due date.
You can renew it at **www.norfolk.gov.uk/libraries**
or by using our free library app. Otherwise you can
phone **0344 800 8020** - please have your library
card and pin ready.
You can sign up for email reminders too.

NORFOLK COUNTY COUNCIL
LIBRARY AND INFORMATION SERVICE

NORFOLK ITEM

3 0129 08548 4104

BBC CHILDREN'S BOOKS

UK I USA I Canada I Ireland I Australia
India I New Zealand I South Africa

BBC Children's Books are published by Puffin Books,
part of the Penguin Random House group of companies
whose addresses can be found at global.penguinrandomhouse.com.
www.penguin.co.uk   www.puffin.co.uk   www.ladybird.co.uk

First published 2021
001

Written by Louie Stowell
Illustrated by Robin Boyden
Copyright © BBC, 2021

Text design by Mandy Norman
Printed and bound in Great Britain by Clays Ltd, Elcograf S.p.A.

The authorized representative in the EEA is Penguin Random House Ireland,
Morrison Chambers, 32 Nassau Street, Dublin DO2 YH68

A CIP catalogue record for this book is available from the British Library

ISBN: 978–1–405–93951–5

All correspondence to:
BBC Children's Books
Penguin Random House Children's UK
One Embassy Gardens, 8 Viaduct Gardens
London SW11 7BW

Penguin Random House is committed to a
sustainable future for our business, our readers
and our planet. This book is made from Forest
Stewardship Council® certified paper.

BBC

DOCTOR WHO

TEAM TARDIS DIARIES

GHOST TOWN

SUSIE DAY

PUFFIN

The Doctor is a Time Lord from the planet Gallifrey. For more than a thousand years she has wandered space and time in her astonishing ship the TARDIS – having adventures, uncovering mysteries, making friends and sometimes saving the world.

The Doctor and her friends Yaz, Ryan and Graham visited the moon of Boda, where the Producers – a peaceful race of aliens – tend the trees of a psychic forest. The forest is the source of psychic paper – an amazing and highly useful material that can read minds, and which has got

the Doctor out of more than one sticky situation.

The Producers gave the Doctor a diary made of psychic paper, which records the adventures of anyone holding it. After a run-in with a gang of space pirates, hired by a shadowy figure known only as the Red Admiral, Graham noticed something strange – the dates in the diary stubbornly refused to move on, as if time were somehow . . . stuck. The Doctor realised that something is terribly wrong, and decides to investigate.

DOWNLOADING MEMORIES . . .

DATELINE:
THURSDAY 31 OCTOBER, 2019
EARTH

You know what I like best about time travel? It makes you notice.

Every incredible thing I've seen, of course. The moonrise over the lava lakes on Prem. How small it was inside the Trojan Horse. This psychic diary, recording everything that happens to me while I'm holding it.

But it's not just the big stuff. Spending three days at home with my family – that's time travel, too. Dad cooking to feed an army 'just in case'. Sonya crying mascara everywhere over Big Sanjay one day and kissing him the next. My hair, growing out of my head.

The Earth spinning through space. The clock ticking. Time travel is happening to all of us, every day.

Or . . . it was. **UNTIL NOW.**

Last night was Halloween. We had six trick-or-treaters: two witches, a whole family of Harry Potters and one Spider-Man. Dad loved it.

Then I got the call from Graham this morning: 'Come round, Yaz, come round right now.' He sounded spooked.

When I got to Graham's house, Ryan and the Doctor were already there. There were fake cobwebs sprayed all over the windows and miniature carved pumpkins placed along the top of the TARDIS, which stood awkwardly in the middle of Graham's living room. Graham shoved the diary into my hands.

And there it was. The date on the page.

Thursday 31 October.

AGAIN.

'But that was yesterday . . .' I said slowly.

'I know!' said Ryan, with a beaming smile. 'Double Halloween. How good is that?' His T-shirt had a skeleton on it.

'No, Mr Pumpkin-head,' said Graham. 'It's not good!'

I looked at the Doctor and saw the worry in her eyes. 'Are we stuck in time, Doctor? How can it be the same day twice?'

'It can't be,' she said firmly, slapping the side of the TARDIS. 'This is a timeship. TARDIS. "T" for time. I know time. And time never just stops.'

'Except it has,' said Ryan. 'It's there in black and white.'

'Everything's normal outside,' I said. 'Well, for this time of year, anyway. Maybe the diary's broken?'

THE PAPER WENT

SCRUNCHY

MY THOUGHTS COMING OUT SMALL **AND STRANGE.**

Psychic paper's easily <u>offended</u>. Best be nice to it, Yaz.

'It is definitely *not* because the diary's broken,' I said very honestly and sincerely and only a little bit louder than normal. 'It's a great diary, isn't it? I love it. We all do.'

'So clever,' said Graham quickly.

'Best diary ever,' added Ryan. 'But, well, if the diary's working fine, then . . .'

'NO!' The Doctor held up her palm. 'We are not stuck in time.'

'All right,' said Graham. 'Let's prove it, yeah? In that timeship of yours.'

The Doctor grinned. **'BRILLIANT!'**

I love it when she does that.

The minute we stepped into the TARDIS, I felt safe.

The Doctor leaped to the console, her hands quick on the controls. 'I'll just go forward one day. Get ahead of the temporal anomaly. Then, we'll figure out where it came from.'

It sounded good to me – till she threw forward the controls.

'WHOA!'

The floor lurched under my feet, sending me flying, then ripped me backwards to hit the inside of the doors. It felt like being in a washing machine. We were spinning wildly, out of control . . .

'HANG ON!' yelled the Doctor, both her arms and one leg hooked on to the console as the whole ship rocked and shuddered.

'What do you think we're doing?' Graham yelled back, his arms wrapped tightly round one of the console's glowing pillars.

The doors flew open behind me with a bang.

'Yaz!' yelled Ryan.

VWURP! VWARP! VWUUUH!

'If I can just . . . reach . . . ' The Doctor was stretching out with one arm, desperately trying to flip a lever that was just beyond her fingertips. 'There!'

With a sudden

I found myself thrown back inside. The TARDIS doors slammed closed behind me and the shaking stopped.

For a minute, I just lay on the floor and tried to catch my breath.

'Everyone OK? Yaz?' The Doctor clambered off the console. She was breathing hard, too.

I nodded, accepting her hand to pull me up.

'What was that?' Ryan rubbed his head where he'd landed on it.

'Fast return. Direct jump back to our starting point. Only way to get you home.' The Doctor's hand slid across the console, palming the door controls. The doors swung open, showing us Graham's living room. 'Right, gang. Team. Fam. It's been great, hasn't it? Brilliant. Now, off you pop. I'll sort this one solo.'

'You what?' said Graham.

The Doctor's too-bright smile faded to grim seriousness. 'Out there? That was the time vortex, and it's broken. That's what's making time stick – like we've reached the end point. I don't like it one bit and neither does the TARDIS. Look.'

She tapped a few controls. The whole console shuddered, as if the ship was shivering. 'Time's stuck on "stop", and without the TARDIS working properly, I've got no idea why. Time virus? Phase loop? Alien life form living off the energy potentiality of parallel universes? Whatever it is, I won't risk trying to take this ship even a millisecond forward till it's sorted. That means I've got to go back: get behind the problem and catch it up.

'If you come with me, with time stopped like this, I can't promise you'll come home, back to your time, ever. So, you can leave now. No guilt, no blame.' The Doctor nodded towards the open doors.

I couldn't believe it. I actually felt kind of angry with her.

'Hey! You've never promised that we'll come home,' I said. 'No one knows the future – not you, not anyone. So we might get nobbled by some alien time-monster thing while travelling? I might get hit by a car, here, tomorrow. Doesn't mean I never leave the house. We chose to do this. With you.'

'You're not ditching us, Doc,' Graham added. 'We can help!'

Ryan rubbed his head again. 'Double Halloween, I like. Nothing but Halloween? Reckon even I'd get bored with that. If time's stuck, I want to help put it right. We all do.'

'Team TARDIS,' I said. Graham and Ryan both nodded.

'All right! I was just checking!' The Doctor grinned as she palmed the doors closed again.

Love a bit of team bonding!!

The Doctor ran her hands over the console, sending lights flashing and read-outs scrolling before our eyes. 'I'll make it fun, I promise! Maybe. I'll try. No hobgoblins! Or slime. No more being sucked out into space. Probably.

'Now, come on, twenty-first-century Earth: what have you got? Can't go forward. Don't want to go further back than we need to. So, where's left, Yaz?'

'Um,' I said.

'Sideways!' said the Doctor.

'Sideways?' mouthed Graham.

Ryan shrugged.

'What does that mean, Doctor?' I asked.

'Don't know yet.' She gasped. 'Oh yes I do! Tomiko Handa. Brilliant.' She grinned, then rapidly tapped in a new course. 'Sideways. Same time, different place. In this case, six thousand five hundred and nine miles east. To Japan!'

This time, the TARDIS

THRUMMED

to life as if nothing was wrong at all.

I'll admit it: I was pretty excited about going to Japan. The nearest I'd got was eating sushi off a conveyor belt at Sonya's thirteenth birthday party. I pictured the bright lights and skyscrapers of Tokyo . . . going to a tea ceremony . . . pink blossom blowing across a beautiful ornamental garden . . .

'Nearly there,' said the Doctor, as the rhythmic bowing of the time rotors began to slow. 'I'm just going to offset us from the original course. We'd better land above ground, so the TARDIS vibrations don't disturb the lake.'

'What lake?' asked Ryan.

'The lake of one hundred per cent pure water inside the Super-K neutrino emission detector!'

'Oh, that lake,' said Graham.

I shrugged back at him, as my Tokyo and pink-blossom dreams blew away.

'Doctor, are we going to some secret underground base?' I asked, as the TARDIS materialised.

'Not exactly.' She opened the doors. 'We're going to – Oh!'

It wasn't a secret base. It wasn't a lake.

It wasn't Japan, either.

We'd landed on a road lined with old wooden buildings that were covered in peeling paint. Before us stood a weathered road sign.

DUMPS WELCOME TO

~~GREENSVILLE~~

THE SMARTEST OIL TOWN
IN TEXAS

'Texas? What happened to Japan?' asked Graham, as the Doctor held the sonic out to test the air.

'I was looking forward to ramen,' Ryan said sadly.

'Now, strictly speaking, I didn't program a course to Japan,' confessed the Doctor. 'I used a bioprint stored in the TARDIS databanks to program a course to Tomiko Handa.'

'Who's that?' I asked.

'Doctor Tomiko Handa? She's a scientist. Brilliant. Nearly as clever as me. That's why her bioprint's in the TARDIS,' she explained, as we hurried after her. 'She has the kind of brain I knew I might find useful again one day.'

'And that Special-K neutron lake thingy?' asked Ryan.

'The Super-Kamiokande neutrino emission detector,' said the Doctor. 'Super-K for short. It's amazing, Ryan! Like all the brilliance of the Large Hadron Collider, only a thousand times more beautiful. A neutrino is a subatomic particle. You can't feel it, you can't see it, but tens of billions of them are flowing towards Earth right now from the sun. It's like there's some invisible electromagnetic high wire strung between them – a constant flow.

'The Super-K team figured out why we couldn't detect some of the neutrinos – because they kept changing what they were like. The team got a Nobel Prize for that. I bought them a massive cake. Lemon. Really thick frosting.'

Yum!
It's really delicious too!

'So Tomiko Handa's going to help us fix the time-being-stuck problem?' asked Graham.

'That's the idea. If time's being affected by a massive shift in gravitational activity, or if there's a cosmic event that's triggered this . . . If there's a point of origin, Tomiko can find it. Or she could in the Super-K. She must have moved here. Can't imagine why, though. That was her dream job.'

I had my dream job, back in Sheffield: police officer. Helping people; doing good work. But when I had the choice I still stayed with the Doctor. I reckon there's lots of reasons people change direction.

'Greensville, the smartest oil town in Texas,' said Graham slowly. 'That's what the sign said, right? Well, before someone vandalised it, anyway.'

'You need pumps for oil,' said Ryan. 'Pumps and drills.'

We could see for miles across the flat, dusty land beyond the shabby little town. There were no pumps working oil up from below, and no processing plants or pipelines. Just a long row of shiny metal fencing in the distance, to protect, well, nothing at all. Just more dusty scrubland.

It didn't look smart, either.

We walked along an improbably new-looking road, between two rows of old shacks. Half the buildings we passed were boarded up, or had dark, empty windows with cracked and broken glass. The rest were deserted. The cobwebs here were for real. Greensville was a forgotten place, filled with actual haunted houses.

'Oil runs out, you know,' said Graham bleakly. 'I bet that's what happened here.'

Graham sighed and went on, 'Town gets built while the money's flowing, then, when the good stuff runs out, everyone leaves. Just like the California gold rush in the 1850s. And this is what gets left behind: a ghost town.'

The Doctor grabbed my wrist as a low whistling sound came from nowhere.

The wind lifted, sending the old buildings up ahead creaking. Doors banged. Windows rattled.

It was sunny, but suddenly I felt chilled cold.

'Doc,' murmured Graham.

From behind the TARDIS came a terrible sound. Wet, heavy breaths. Weighty, dragging footsteps.

'Get behind me,' whispered the Doctor.

She brandished the sonic, frantically trying to get a reading before the thing, whatever it was, could reach us.

When it appeared it was horrifying. A shaggy, matted, loping beast, with black fur and a head that hung at a sickening angle. Its eyes were glassy as it flailed one long limb towards us, and –

Then its head fell off.

'Ah, rats,' said a perfectly human-sounding voice.

The horrifying beast stood up straight and the head of a young girl popped out of the top. It was just a girl in a costume: a cheap gorilla suit.

'Halloween,' breathed Ryan, relieved.

'Ella Jane Baker, you get that costume off right now!' yelled a voice from inside a weathered

wooden building. The house was falling down like the rest of the town, but I could see curtains at the clean windows, and fresh flowers on the windowsill.

A woman emerged, smartly dressed and carrying a briefcase. 'I told you, if you want to skip school to help decorate for the trick-or-treat parade tonight, you're going to work, not monkey around!'

'Gorilla's an ape, Mommy,' murmured Ella Jane, scooping up her fallen gorilla head.

Her mother jumped when she saw us. 'Oh! Well, good day to you. Don't see many strangers around here.'

She sounded like no strangers was just how she liked it. I could see her hand tightening on the briefcase handle.

A young guy in grimy overalls appeared on the porch of the old shack opposite. He was dragging a huge box of Halloween decorations filled with skeletons and electric lights. When he saw us, he looked even more unwelcoming than Ella Jane's mother.

'These people bothering you, Tara?'

'Not us,' said the Doctor cheerfully. 'We're no bother. Hello!'

The young guy looked sour.

'You're just a little surprising is all,' said Tara, clutching her briefcase even tighter. 'What – what brings you to Greensville?'

'You'll be looking for the Institute. It's a couple miles up the road,' said Ella Jane. 'Right, Mom?' She looked at her mother, a glint of mischief in her eye. 'Mom works there. She'll show you the way.'

Tara shook her head. 'Sorry,' she said, backing away. 'If you're looking for work, there's really nothing going. And you'd need a security permit to enter the area. Better just move along now. Try some place else.'

Tara disappeared behind her house. Moments later, a sleek silver car spun out on to the road and sped away.

'You heard the lady.' The young guy eyeballed us from his porch before heading back indoors.

'That was dead weird,' said Ryan.

> Not very friendly, are they?

'A security permit just to get into the office?' said Graham. 'Where exactly does your mum work?'

'The Savior Institute,' said Ella Jane, rolling her eyes. 'Whatever that is. It's all some big secret. We used to live in the city, where she was an engineer. Then, she hears about this fancy new job in her old home town, and suddenly she's telling me how we can move back into Grandpa's old house, how it's all going to be this amazing new life for us two. Look at this place! The trick-or-treat parade's the only time of year that old Greensville comes back to life. Everybody else lives up in the new town, now – through the fence.' She waved a hand up the road.

Far in the distance, the road led directly to a gate in the fence. As we watched, Tara's silver car reached the gate, and a pair of guards swung it open. Once inside, her car disappeared.

The Savior Institute?
Sounds interesting . . .

Ella Jane looked at us sideways. 'I bet y'all know what they do up there, huh? That's why you came here. To stop them.' Her eyes gleamed with excitement.

The young guy poked his head out of the

shack. 'Ella Jane! You come on inside and help, now.'

Ella Jane kicked at the dirt crossly, the gleam in her eyes gone. 'You take care, y'hear?' she said, suddenly serious. 'I mean it. They sure don't like strangers.'

She pulled her gorilla head back on and loped up the porch steps, unable to resist one last

'RWAAAARGH!'

before she went inside.

'I like her,' said the Doctor. 'Love a good

"RWAAAARGH",

'She nearly gave me heart failure,' said Graham.

'Come on, Grandad!' Ryan grinned. 'How can you not love Halloween?'

We walked for a while before we reached the Institute.

Or where it ought to have been, anyway.

The road led us past crumbling old shacks until we came to the tall chain-link fence and the security gate where Ella Jane's mother had entered, which was now closed. The guardhouse was deserted. Through the gate, the road

continued on towards . . . nothing. Just a tiny old building in the middle of nowhere.

Up close, I could hear the fence humming. 'Electrified?' I asked.

'They really don't like strangers,' whispered Ryan. Curious, he reached out with his fingertips.

'Oi!' said Graham. 'Don't touch –'

AAAHHH!

Something ripped the ground apart.

'It wasn't me!' Ryan cried. 'I didn't even touch the fence!'

It happened again as he was scrambling to his feet.

BANG!

BANG!

BANG!

'Someone's shooting at us!' I yelled.

Ryan ran one way, I went the other. The Doctor yanked me to safety behind a low wall.

Graham joined us a second later. 'Who's shooting?' He peered tentatively round the corner.

The Doctor frowned. Then she picked up a handful of dirt and threw it at the fence.

There was another wave of little explosions. It wasn't bullets. There must have been something buried all along the perimeter.

'That fence isn't electric – it's sensory.' The Doctor stood up carefully. 'It's quite clever, really. In a horrible way. Anyone gets near enough and *boom*. But who would want to keep people out that much?'

'Who's asking?' A deep voice came from behind us, shockingly loud.

A man in black fatigues and mirrored sunglasses stepped through the fence. He wore an equipment belt, like the one from my police uniform, with a two-way radio and a baton. Except his belt had a gun, too.

'I got 'em,' he said into his radio, then clipped it back on to his belt. 'Now –'

The Doctor jumped up and cut him off. 'What kind of welcome is that, eh? We came here to visit your Savior Institute, and that's how you say hello?'

'We don't accept visitors, ma'am.'

'You do when it's us. And you will when you've seen our credentials.'

Graham gave me a nervous look. 'What credentials?' he murmured.

I was more worried about Ryan. He was crouching in the shadow of the next building, trying desperately to keep out of sight.

'My colleague here has our letter of introduction. Don't you, Yaz?' said the Doctor, flapping a hand wildly at me behind her back. 'Our letter. Written on a page of very brilliant, best-ever, love-it-to-bits paper.'

'Oh!'

I winced, and tore a page out of the diary.

Sorry, diary!

Needed you to help out with a bit of psychic osmosis.

To whom it may concern,

A deputation from Her Majesty's Government of the United Kingdom has been sent to observe this facility. In the interests of international scientific co-operation and the continuation of the special relationship, you are required to admit these citizens:

– **THE DOCTOR**, scientific advisor to Her Majesty the Queen

– **LIEUTENANT COLONEL YASMIN KHAN**, British Army

– **MR G. O'BRIEN**, private citizen and billionaire entrepreneur

Please extend every courtesy to these guests on US soil. This visit is to remain confidential.

Regards,

It worked perfectly.

Minutes later, we were being driven through the gate in the fence. Towards what? Who knew.

'How did it do that?' I whispered, looking down at the diary with new-found respect.

'Smart stuff, psychic paper,' said the Doctor.

'I'm a billionaire?' murmured Graham, peering over my shoulder at our 'credentials'.

'He must think you look the type,' the Doctor whispered back.

Graham exhaled, puffing out his cheeks. I could tell he was privately pleased. I was, too. Lieutenant colonel sounded a lot better than junior police officer.

'I'm sorry we left Ryan behind,' said the Doctor.

Graham grinned. 'He can finish off his Halloween outfit. He'll be fine.'

The car dropped us off at the tiniest building I'd ever seen. It was a door connected to three walls. And it wasn't like the TARDIS inside: just a hot metal box and a tight squeeze.

Mirror-glasses stayed outside. 'Be patient,' he said. 'It's a long way down. Oh, and . . . none of you are afraid of the dark, right?'

He grinned, showing perfect teeth, and closed the door.

We were

PLUNGED INTO TOTAL DARKNESS.

There was a clanking noise, then suddenly I felt my tummy lift, the way it does on a roller-coaster.

We were in a lift and it was **GOING DOWN – FAST.**

Graham grabbed on to my arm to steady himself. The Doctor was already holding my hand.

We waited in the darkness, breathing together, all the way down.

DIARY DISCONNECTED . . .

SEEKING NEW INPUT . . .

The lift stopped with a jolt, and we toppled over in a clump on the floor.

'**OOF!** Everyone OK?' asked the Doctor.

A sudden bright light came on and left me blinking.

I was lucky to see it at all: the diary, on the floor. It had fallen from Yaz's pocket. I tried to hand it back to her, but she shook her head. 'Reckon a psychic diary is less weird in the pocket of a billionaire.'

I slipped it into my jacket. You don't want to leave something like that just lying around. Not when you've been driven across the desert and sent down a big hole in the ground.

'Best faces on,' whispered the Doctor. 'Most fancy smiles. People who live behind fences are bound to be a bit up themselves.'

When the elevator doors slid open, I was expecting more military types like the one in the shades, but someone else was waiting for us.

At the head of a long, dim corridor was a fella who looked like a friendly wizard.

He was older than me by a good decade or two. He had the wrinkles of a guy who'd seen a lot of sunshine, and the belly of one who'd lived the good life. His white hair was thin on top, but long. It was tied in a skinny ponytail that hung down his back and he had a long beard to match. He wore what I'd call hippy clothes, and Ryan would probably call retro or hipster or something while rolling his eyes.

'William Green Senior,' he said in a broad Texan twang, 'but you can call me Buck – everybody does.'

He held out his hand, shaking each of ours in turn with a firm, warm grip. 'It's an honour, ma'am. And you, ma'am. Hello, sir. It's my pleasure to welcome you to the Savior Institute. Step this way.'

The corridor was like a life-size family album.

I recognised it right away: grief. This Buck fella was mourning. But – well, in my house, there's pictures of Grace, sure. But not that many. Not that big. This was just a little bit creepy.

There's no right way to remember them, is there? The people we've lost. They were all different. Special in their own way. So's grief.

'Maddy Green. My inspiration,' Buck explained as we walked. 'She's the reason for all this. My baby girl. I was an oil man for the longest time. Big Buck Green, the richest man in Texas. Built a whole town on the black stuff – even named it after myself. Thought I was It. You can get a little lost when you're rich, you know. Spiritually, I mean. You'll know all about that, Mr O'Brien.' Buck clapped me on the shoulder sympathetically.

'Oh yeah,' I said quickly. 'Being a billionaire. It's . . . rough.'

Yaz struggled to hide a giggle.

'She was a firecracker from the cradle, that girl,' Buck said, gesturing to another photo. Teenage Maddy in a plaid shirt. She stood beside Buck with her arms folded, an edge to her smile.

'I made some choices back in those boomtown days that Maddy didn't agree with,' Buck continued. 'I used to think it was just hippy stuff, you know? Save the whales, save the bees, weave hemp underwear and grow your own toothpaste. We fought. We didn't part on good terms. And . . . well, I thought she'd grow out of it. Thought I had all the time in the world for her to come round and see things my way.'

I knew that feeling, too. Regret.

We stopped walking in front of one last huge portrait, a painting this time.

Yaz's eyebrows shot up. I could see why: it was cheesy as anything. But Buck pressed his palm against his chest, and I could see what it meant to him.

'She passed. Two years gone now. And I was left with nothing – nothing that mattered, anyhow. The oil had run dry, people were leaving the town. Everything I'd built was crumbling to dust – when I would've traded it all for one more day with my girl.'

'I'm sorry,' said the Doctor softly.

'Me too, mate.' I touched Buck's arm.

'Thank you, ma'am. Sir.' He dipped his

head before the portrait as if in prayer, then straightened up and set his shoulders back. 'That's when I said to myself, "Enough. She ain't here? Let's make it like she is. Give her a legacy to be proud of." And that's how the Savior Institute was born.' He gestured ahead, towards a soft, golden glow.

We followed him along the corridor. Other doors and corridors snaked off, but I was drawn towards that glow.

The corridor ended in a vast cavern. A high ceiling had been carved into the rock, and the wide room was walled with read-outs and control panels, computers and screens. Before us was a viewing gallery, lined with thick glass.

'Oh yes,' breathed the Doctor. She hurried forward and pressed her hands against the glass. I followed, and waited for my eyes to adjust to the brightness.

'This is an exact replica of the Super-K neutrino detector in Japan,' said the Doctor, her eyes shining in the golden light.

The Doc had said the Super-K was beautiful, but I'd had no idea. It was mad. How could a thing that detected neutrinos – whatever they were – look like the inside of a Christmas bauble?

And how was it going to help us unfreeze time?

The sound of pounding feet headed our way, followed by an angry voice. 'Buck Green! You wanna tell me why I'm the last person to know we've got visitors?'

A woman emerged from a corridor. Her dark hair was tied back in a messy knot and she had what looked like a soup stain on her T-shirt. She was short but solid, and about the same age as the Doc.

Well . . . maybe not *exactly* the same age, Graham.

'Tomiko!' There was a yelp as the Doctor flung her arms around the woman.

'Excuse me?' she said, struggling to escape the Doctor's grip. 'I don't hug my cat that tight, let alone a stranger. Who is in my lab. Without my permission. And who brought some friends. Who the heck are these people, Buck?'

The Doctor stood back, crestfallen.

Buck stepped awkwardly between them. 'Hey, Doctor Handa. These are our very special guests from the United Kingdom. Sent by the Queen!' he added in a giddy whisper.

'Thought you were old mates, Doc?' I murmured as Buck introduced us. Tomiko shook our hands stiffly.

'It's been a while,' the Doctor whispered back. 'Years, probably. People change; look different. You know how it is.'

I didn't. Baldy Jon from the buses once came back from his holidays with a mop of brown hair like a Beatle, and I never missed a beat. I just called him Wiggy Jon from then on. People don't change that much – not so much that you wouldn't recognise a mate. But the Doc looked so sad that I didn't like to say anything.

Besides, there wasn't time. A red light started to flash on the wall next to the viewing gallery. A low but insistent warning alarm began to buzz.

'See?' said Tomiko, flinging her arms in the air. 'This is why we don't invite tourists. These are delicate instruments. I'm doing science here, Buck! Big, proper science for grown-ups!'

BUZZ.

BUZZ.

BUZZ.

BUZZ.

BUZZ.

BUZZ.

BUZZ.

BUZZ.

'We didn't touch anything,' said Yaz quickly. 'It's not us. Right, Doctor?'

'I wouldn't even know how to mess this thing up,' I added.

The Doctor dashed to the gallery and scanned the lake below with her sonic. She squinted at the read-out. 'Not good,' she said.

'Not good at all,' agreed Tomiko by her side, watching the ripples on the water. 'Wait. Is that a sonic screwdriver?'

'Yep.'

'That girl – she called you Doctor.'

'Yep.'

'You're the Doctor.' Tomiko blinked. She looked the Doc up and down as though she was trying to catch up with a million thoughts at once.

The Doc grinned, preening under all that scrutiny. 'I've changed a bit.'

Tomiko nodded slowly, then smirked. 'Your dress sense has definitely improved.'

Before the Doctor could respond, the sonic buzzed. 'Oh! Lake contamination. I'm really sorry. I swear it wasn't us. But –'

'Come on,' said Tomiko. 'This room's all flashy lights and nonsense. The good stuff's in my personal lab.'

They ran off, then Tomiko reappeared, poking her head out from a doorway. 'Turn off that alarm, Buck, for pity's sake. People are trying to save the world around here.'

BUZZ.

BUZZ.

BUZZ.

BUZZ.

BU–

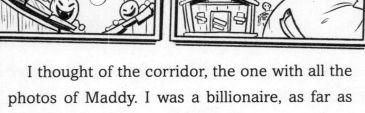

I thought of the corridor, the one with all the photos of Maddy. I was a billionaire, as far as Buck knew. I reckoned that meant I could ask whatever I liked. 'Not being funny, Mr Green, but I don't get it. You said your daughter inspired all this. How does that detector thing fit in?'

Buck wasn't offended. He beamed, like I'd given him the best opportunity of his life. 'Walk this way, my friend.' He put his arm round me.

'The lieutenant colonel's coming, too,' grumbled Yaz, running to catch us up.

Buck led Yaz and me deeper into the Institute. We trekked down another dim corridor that led to a sort of space-age boardroom with a wall of television screens, all showing different video feeds.

'Look, there's Ryan!' I said.

'Is that Tara, Ella Jane's mum?' Yaz peered closely at another screen, showing some kind of warehouse or factory.

Buck gestured and all the monitors flicked off at once.

'The Savior Institute,' he said grandly. At his words, another huge screen lit up and a sort of mini-movie began.

BUT NOT EVERYONE LOVES THIS PLANET
AS MUCH AS MADDY DID . . .

LANDFILL PRODUCES TOXIC GASES.
RECYCLING ISN'T ENOUGH TO FIX THE PROBLEM.

HYDROGEN SULPHIDE

AMMONIA

METHANE

CARBON DIOXIDE

YOU'RE POISONING YOUR OWN HOME!

'So far, so obvious,' said Buck. The display changed to show a CGI video of his daughter, Maddy. She was walking through a wheat field and smiling peacefully. Then, the outline of Maddy swirled into a new shape, like a peapod that was lying flat. It floated in nothingness. As we watched, it sprouted tendrils that grew into slim wings, and tiny buds that grew into engines.

Yaz understood first. 'It's a ship.'

'A spaceship,' I said.

They don't all look like the TARDIS, you know!

'The first solar-wind spacecraft in history,' said Buck, with awe in his voice.

'And the single solution to this planet's environmental troubles. We can recycle. We can switch to alternative fuels. But fact is, we're wasteful. You can't change that overnight. You know how many people campaigned against me about fossil fuels? Millions. You know how many campaign against methane gas? A handful. It's garbage. No one gets mad at garbage – they just want it to be taken away.

'So that's what I'm doing. We've got the answer up there among the stars: the sun. A big old ball of energy that'll burn up anything that gets too close. Our very own garbage disposal. All we gotta do is get it there.'

He'd lost me. What did that have to do with the Christmas-bauble lake?

Yaz was baffled, too. 'OK. But how are you going to get it all to the sun?'

'That's where the neutrinos come in!' said Buck. 'Billions of them are travelling between the Earth and the sun, right now.'

I snapped my fingers. 'Gotcha. Like the Doc said: an electromagnetic high wire.'

Buck nodded. 'Now, I'm no scientist; I can't claim to understand the details. But one day, someone sent me an article about these amazing neutrino discoveries. So, I went to Japan and I explained what I wanted to Doctor Handa. Once I offered her complete control of her very own neutrino detector, she signed up right away. She's mapping a path through the solar winds and finding the moment the neutrino density peaks. We're gonna ride that solar wind all the way to the sun. Our ship's one of a kind. I call her the *Maddy*.'

'You named a spaceship after your daughter . . . and it's to take garbage into space?' Yaz's face was a picture.

'I figure she'll forgive me, Colonel. After all, it was her idea.'

The screen flickered to show us a new image: a drawing.

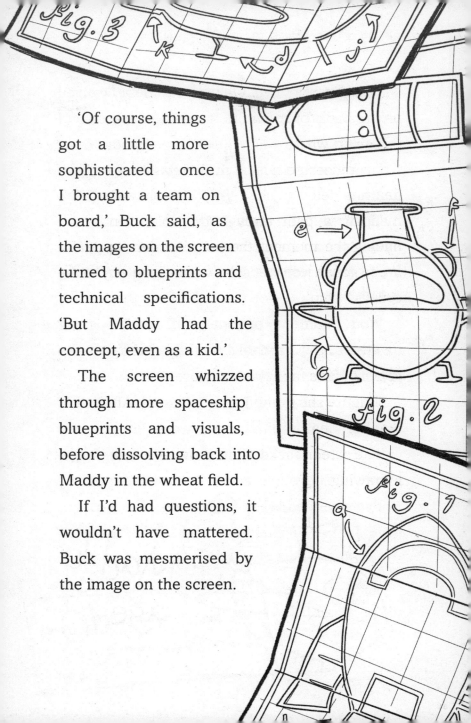

'Of course, things got a little more sophisticated once I brought a team on board,' Buck said, as the images on the screen turned to blueprints and technical specifications. 'But Maddy had the concept, even as a kid.'

The screen whizzed through more spaceship blueprints and visuals, before dissolving back into Maddy in the wheat field.

If I'd had questions, it wouldn't have mattered. Buck was mesmerised by the image on the screen.

I caught Yaz's eye. We both stood and walked to the bank of monitors, as if checking one of the displays.

'You thinking what I'm thinking?' murmured Yaz.

'That we get away from Uncle Buck and have a proper look around? I mean . . . you are a lieutenant colonel. You're not used to *taking* orders.'

'And you're a billionaire. If you're going to invest, you probably want to check out the merchandise, right?'

I knew one thing: I didn't trust Buck. People manage grief in all kinds of ways, but here we were in his secret underground lair, listening to him tell us his plans in way too much detail.

I've watched a lot of movies. Buck might have looked like Dumbledore, but I know a supervillain when I see one.

I do love a **villain** monologue though, always very helpful.

It wasn't long before we had a chance to escape.

Another alarm sounded, this one more insistent than the last. Purple lights flashed across the ceiling.

BUZZ!

BUZZ!

BUZZ!

BUZZ!

BUZZ!

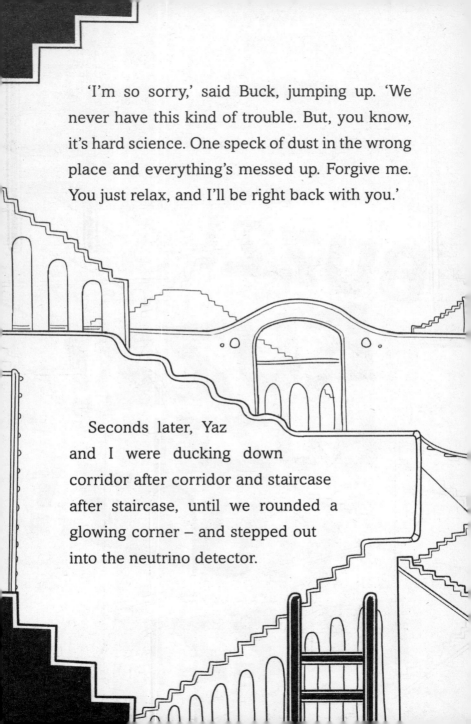

'I'm so sorry,' said Buck, jumping up. 'We never have this kind of trouble. But, you know, it's hard science. One speck of dust in the wrong place and everything's messed up. Forgive me. You just relax, and I'll be right back with you.'

Seconds later, Yaz and I were ducking down corridor after corridor and staircase after staircase, until we rounded a glowing corner – and stepped out into the neutrino detector.

Close up, it was extraordinary. I've seen a lot with the Doc, of course. The triple skies of Cooi. Cleopatra's burnished ship gliding up the Nile. But this lake was something else. As we got nearer, you could tell that something was happening – like a thrum or a throb. The surface of the whole lake was tingling, like my tea when Ryan plays his music too loud. The golden glow reflected by the thousands of lightbulbs above made the whole surface seem alive.

Alive, and getting more so.

It wasn't my imagination. With every step closer to the lake, the ripples grew stronger.

'Is it meant to do that?' whispered Yaz. She crouched down and reached her fingertips towards the surface.

'Yaz!' The Doctor's voice echoed from a speaker, filled with warning.

I stared around in alarm. She was high above us, on a sealed glass viewing platform on the other side of the lake. Tomiko was at her side. 'Don't touch that  water! It's one hundred per cent pure – needs to stay uncontaminated! And pure doesn't mean healthy and delicious. It means it'll leach every mineral in your skin from your body!'

Yaz fell backwards. I stepped back, too. The ripples faded.

Weird.

I stepped forward again.

The ripples grew stronger.

I wasn't imagining it: the ripples, the **THRUMMING** energy.

It was . . . me?

But how?

Now that is interesting! Very, very interesting.

The ripples were turning into waves, sloshing up against the edges of the lake.

I took a few more hasty steps back, but it didn't make a difference this time.

'You need to get out of there,' the Doctor urged. 'Now! Go!'

Yaz ran past me. 'Graham, come on!' she called.

But it was too late.

The waves were growing, swelling and rising like a tidal surge.

Then the lake exploded.

WHOOSH!
SPLOSH!
SPLEESH!

There wasn't another word for it. The water shot up in the air like a bomb had gone off, then smashed back down again with a roar, soaking me head to toe. The glowing golden lightbulbs overhead shattered and glass rained down. There was a moment of pure darkness.

I scrabbled about on my hands and knees till I found Yaz in the dark. She yelped when I grabbed her ankle.

The emergency lighting flickered on, emitting a faint green glow.

'What's it doing?' whispered Yaz, staring.

Now the lake was churning and swirling. A whirlpool formed, foaming and savage. Then, with a sudden loud sucking noise, the water drained away. It wasn't slow like when a bath drains, but all at once, as if whatever was underneath had just disappeared.

'Stay back!' warned the Doctor.

I didn't need telling twice, but it made no difference. The soaked ground where I'd been splashed began to crumble.

Then, the ground beneath our feet, it just

FELL AWAY.

AND WE FELL WITH IT.

'Graham? **GRAHAM!**'

My back hurt. I'd landed on something solid and smooth, like rock, but it was covered with gritty earth and broken glass. I figured I must've been knocked out for a second or two.

I could feel hands patting me. I clocked pretty quickly that I was OK, but that maybe the person asking wasn't.

'Well, my ears are definitely working,' I mumbled.

Yaz let out a big sigh of relief. 'Phew. Thought you'd done yourself in and left me to it!'

When I opened my eyes, I understood why she'd sounded so panicked.

Everything was black.

PERFECT BLACK DARKNESS.

We were deep underground before we fell. How could we have fallen even further?

My mind drifted back to the old sign on the road. *Greensville: the smartest oil town in Texas.*

Oil well. We were down an old oil well. Who knew how deep?

I took a moment to be glad that Ryan wasn't with us. He'd hate this. Then I took a moment to wish he was, just in case this was it, and we weren't going to make it.

That was enough of that.

'Right. So, what next?' I tried to sound breezy.

'I could try climbing?' suggested Yaz. 'I've felt around us. It's narrow, like an upright tunnel. The walls are pretty crumbly, but I reckon if I brace my back on one side and my feet on the other –'

'Ooh! That would've been great. I'm a bit sad I've rescued you now.' The Doctor's voice floated down from above.

A faint green light appeared overhead.

In the glow I could see a platform lowering towards us, and the Doctor's face hanging off the edge.

'Hello! Sorry about the wait. Had to rig this thing to go deep enough. Stop now, Tomiko!' she called up.

The platform jolted to a stop a few feet above my head.

'You'll need a wash after that soaking, Graham. You might be a bit itchy. And your hair might fall out, sorry. I'll have to get you out one at a time. This platform can't carry more than two – Oh.'

The Doctor's breeziness vanished and her face went stiff. She reached for her sonic. It buzzed alarmingly as she scanned the rock underneath us.

When she looked at the read-out, her face darkened.

'What is it?' said Yaz.

'Just – don't move, either of you. And don't panic.'

'Thanks, Doc. Can we have a clue what we're not panicking about?' I asked.

The Doctor smiled unconvincingly. 'Right. So, when you fell, you didn't land on rock, or earth, or compacted oil, or anything that you might expect to find at the bottom of an oil well.

What you're actually lying on right now is the hull of a massive Katz animator ship.'

'Massive cats?' said Yaz.

'You'd think they'd be softer,' I said.

The Doctor grinned. 'Massive cats would be brilliant! I love cats. But this is Katz. **K-A-T-Z**. They're a bioengineering syndicate from Pangamma Seven. Geniuses. They invented something called the animator virus. It's like a chameleon, turned up to eleven. It rearranges the molecular structure of matter to reconstruct whatever it's been programmed to. Amazing, really. It's got loads of uses: growing new limbs, rebuilding cities after wars or natural disasters . . .'

'Sounds brilliant,' said Yaz. 'What's it doing down here?'

'No idea.' The Doctor shook her head. 'It doesn't make sense. Even if the ship had crashed on Earth, it would've rebuilt itself and gone home. What are the chances of it being right here, directly below the detector? Along with my old mate Tomiko, who shouldn't be here either. *And* a mysterious underground base – the kind I just love to nose around.'

'Do you think it was put here for you to find?' said Yaz, puzzled. 'You didn't even know you were coming here till this morning.'

The Doctor frowned. 'I didn't even know I was coming here while I was coming here. All this: it's like it *was* waiting for us to find it. Like it was put here for us . . . for me.'

I'd had a knock on the head, so I couldn't be sure, but I could've sworn a butterfly flew past my face. Remember the butterfly from that business with the Producers on Boda?

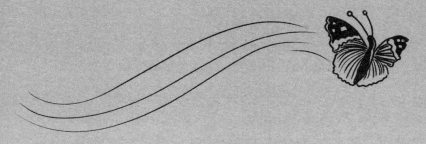

Suddenly, the surface beneath me began to **HUM**.

'Doc,' I whispered.

'Right.' She inhaled sharply. 'Priorities. Yaz, get up here. We'll get you out first. Graham, sit tight. One minute, that's all. Just one. OK?'

'Go,' I breathed, trying to stay as still as possible.

Yaz swung herself up on to the platform. The Doctor called up to Tomiko and the platform slowly rose.

As I lay there, the ache in my back started to fade. Then it vanished completely, along with the little cuts I'd received all over when the lightbulbs had shattered. My head felt clear. My thoughts felt faster.

The animator virus. It was reconstructing my matter and putting me back together.

I wasn't going to be itchy. I wasn't going to be Wiggy Graham. In fact, I felt amazing. I didn't even need to wait for the Doc.

I could climb up like Yaz had said. I felt strong.

SUPERPOWERED.

I sat up, pushing myself on to my knees. The smooth surface beneath my palms grew warm. Then, it dissolved into millions of shiny black fragments, like beads of glass or beetle backs. They rippled under my hands, flowing over one another, to form a face.

My face.

And they didn't stop there.

The face grew, becoming life-size. It was getting **BIGGER –**

BIGGER
BY
THE
SECOND.

'GRAHAM!' The Doctor had descended on her platform. **'JUMP!'**

I leaped aboard and we shot back up the well.

'What is that?' cried Tomiko, as the Doc and I scrambled through the broken glass windows of the viewing gallery.

'It's . . . me,' I said. 'Well, not me. I don't know. It's not my fault!'

'That's the trouble with Katz technology,' said the Doctor grimly. 'Reads a human body like a blueprint, puts it back together: amazing. There's just one problem. When they invented it, they forgot to tell it how to stop!'

It – I – was still growing, rising up out of the old oil well. Within a few seconds, my massive head was level with the viewing gallery.

Huge, blank eyes swung our way.

'RUN!' yelled the Doctor.

I sprinted after Yaz and Tomiko. Too fast. My feet skidded on the broken glass, sending me flying, and the diary tumbled from my jacket pocket.

I know I should expect all sorts now that I travel with the Doctor. Big spiders. Planets made of smoke. The feast of the Terminal Jousters, where I ate a sort of prawn that tasted like minty bananas.

Loved that prawn!

Even so, I didn't expect Greensville to suddenly start spouting black stuff out of the ground, like all the dried-up oil had suddenly come back to say hello.

I definitely didn't expect to find the diary spouted up with it.

And, after I picked up the diary, I really, really didn't expect what I saw when I stood back up: Graham.

GRANDAD.

Only he was about ninety feet tall and made out of that weird black stuff. He climbed up out of the ground and stomped his massive feet towards the busy old town, where the Halloween trick-or-treat parade was about to begin.

Me and Ella Jane had been having a great time till then.

Turned out the gorilla girl was the kind of kid that Nan warned me off, and I'd always ended up being friends with anyway. Kids that were always in trouble, with me following along and saying sorry afterwards.

Trouble just finds some people, you know.

Ella Jane had been happy to fill me in on Greensville, too. How her mum had grown up there, back in the boomtown days when the oil was flowing. Of course, it had only made real money for the guy at the top: Big Buck Green.

You have to wonder about a bloke who names a town after himself, right?

And then he'd built a whole new town, complete with houses, a school and stores, as well as jobs for anyone who wanted them. A private little world called New Greensville, like the old days had never happened. Ella Jane said it was creepy and I was right there with her.

There was one day in the year when even Ella Jane liked living in Greensville, though. 31 October – **HALLOWEEN**. When you were allowed to be weird and muck about, and just be a kid.

Nan hated that British people had started doing Halloween more and more. I think she was worried about what could happen to me, a black kid, knocking on the door of some stranger in a nice part of town. She worried I wasn't safe, and she was probably right, but she made out like that wasn't the real reason. She said British people shouldn't get so excited about some stupid American holiday.

That's really sad, Ryan. Grace was wrong about where it comes from, though! Carving faces in veg? That's Scottish!

Ella Jane understood, though. She got her mum's make-up and some torn old clothes, and she did me a scary zombie look with scars and blood made out of lipstick.

Then we'd hung around eating candy corn while we watched everyone arrive from the new town for the trick-or-treat parade.

Until giant Graham showed up.

Right there, in the middle of the parade, the giant Graham stomped its huge feet and swung its massive head this way and that. There were a few cheers for the amazing Halloween costume.

Suddenly, more black stuff shot up out of the earth. It looked like liquid, but when it fell it shattered into millions of glossy, glasslike beads. They snaked across the ground and joined the enormous body of Graham, making him grow even bigger.

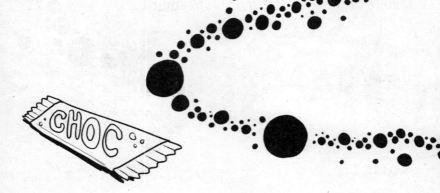

'OK, I guess that wasn't totally lame,' said a kid dressed as a Ghostbuster.

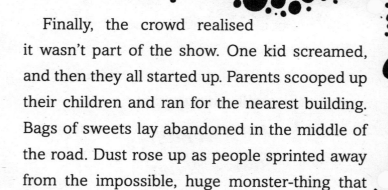

Finally, the crowd realised it wasn't part of the show. One kid screamed, and then they all started up. Parents scooped up their children and ran for the nearest building. Bags of sweets lay abandoned in the middle of the road. Dust rose up as people sprinted away from the impossible, huge monster-thing that had erupted in the middle of their town.

'Ella Jane!' yelled Tara, running towards us on the porch. 'You get inside the house, now!'

'What is it?' Ella clutched her gorilla head tightly as we sheltered behind dangling plastic skeletons.

I swallowed hard. I didn't want to answer. I didn't know how.

Was Graham in there, like Bruce Banner was inside the Hulk?

Maybe I could reason with him.

I had to try.

You, Ryan Sinclair, are a wonderful human being.

'Stay here,' I said, stepping down on to the main street. I squared my shoulders. I looked up, and up.

Giant Graham stared back down at me.

'Hey! Graham?' I cleared my throat. 'Grandad? It's Ryan. It's me. I want to help you, yeah? How can I help you?'

It lowered its head towards me.

I gave it a little wave, feeling hopeful.

The hope didn't last long. Giant Graham's hands began to grow extra fingers and long strings of shiny black stuff, like an army of beetles, poured across the ground.

People screamed. I probably did, too.

The beetle things moved fast. Strings of them flowed from Graham and scurried across the road towards the nearby stores.

They covered a row of carved pumpkin heads on the porch of the hardware store, wrapping the faces in black. They swarmed the dangling skeletons hanging from the roof.

And then, somehow, they brought the decorations to life.

The pumpkin heads grew weird triangular eyes that blinked in their carved eye sockets. Their wide mouths filled with real white teeth, shaped like **JAGGED** points.

The skeletons grew veins and arteries, muscle and flesh. They reached up with their half-finished arms, unhooking themselves from where they dangled.

The pumpkins snapped their **SHARP TEETH**.

The skeletons took their first, awkward steps, as their skin was still growing, unsteady on too-spindly limbs that weren't made to be real.

'Gross,' said Ella Jane, making a barf face. 'Wait, what are they doing?'

'They're learning,' I said.

You could see it happening. They were looking out of their skulls with their new eyes, seeing people dressed as cats and firefighters and cowboys who were all running and screaming.

So, they started to run and scream, too.

It was chaos, like the worst horror movie ever.

You know when you think something can't get worse? Don't do that, because it can.

It happened in an instant, and I kicked myself for not seeing it coming.

Once the beetle things had done their job on the pumpkin heads and the skeletons, bringing them to life (or something like it), they started on real people.

I heard a scream, sharper than the rest, as the glossy black-beetle shapes flowed over Ella's gorilla costume and swarmed up to her head.

The gorilla's fur grew glossier. The dangling arms grew broader and stronger. The head stopped being a too-big mask with fake plastic teeth balancing on Ella Jane's head. It became the face of a real beast, snorting and staring, with dark brown eyes that were filled with fear.

'ELLA, NO!' I shouted.

THE GORILLA ROARED.

IT RAISED ITS FISTS AND BEAT THE GROUND.

IT BARED ITS **TEETH**, WHICH WERE NOW REAL, AND VERY, VERY **SHARP**.

'GET BACK!' came a yell.

There was a humming in the air. The gorilla seemed to shudder in front of me and, a second later, it was just a costume again. To make sure, I pulled at the head and it came off in my hand, revealing a wide-eyed Ella Jane.

'Good old sonic,' said the Doctor, breathlessly running up to us. 'Just took me a minute to get the calibration set. You all right?'

Ella Jane blinked, staring down at the gorilla mask in my hands. 'What just –'

'I'll explain later. Hiya, Ryan, you OK?' The Doctor aimed the sonic at a little girl, crying at the now-alive second head that had grown out of her shoulder. In an instant, it turned back into a doll's head.

'Yeah . . . no . . . yeah,' I said.

No shame if you're not OK, Ryan – that was scary stuff. If you have nightmares, you just shout. I'll be there in a heartbeat with a cup of cocoa. I promise

'Whoa.' Yaz ran up to join us. 'This is . . .'

'More Halloween than I wanted,' I said grimly.

Then Graham arrived: the real one, with a Japanese woman in a scruffy T-shirt beside him.

'It's not my fault,' he said in a faint voice.

'We know!' said Yaz wearily.

'It's not you, Graham!' shouted the Doctor, still wielding her sonic in the crowd. Skeletons fell to the ground. Pumpkin heads became vegetables again. Anyone who had grown a tail was once again tailless and back in costume.

I took a second to breathe.

'Is it over? Hi, by the way. Tomiko Handa.' The woman in the scruffy T-shirt held out her hand. 'I'm having the worst day ever. How are you?'

'Ryan. Same, I reckon.'

'Oi! I'm doing my best.' The Doctor grinned as she zapped the last of the pumpkins back to normality. 'Now then, matey.' She looked up at giant Graham. 'What are we going to do about you?'

Giant Graham's face swung our way. Its expression was blank but its intention was clear as it reached out its arms. Black stuff cascaded from its hands.

'OH NO YOU DON'T!'

The Doctor brandished the sonic, and the glossy beads retreated back into the monster's long, stretched fingers. She kept sending sonic pulses into the massive body.

'It's too big!' Her face scrunched up with frustration. 'I can keep it here and keep it still, but the minute I stop it's just going to start up again. Oh, why didn't the Katz invent an off-switch?'

'What do we do?' Graham looked guiltier than ever.

'We need to contain it,' the Doctor said.

'The TARDIS?' suggested Yaz.

'No way am I letting that Katz tech anywhere near my ship. Then it'd be even more dangerous.'

'If only Buck's ship worked,' said Tomiko.

'Eh?' I tried to picture a boat moored somewhere in this dustbowl of a town.

But Yaz gasped, her eyes bright.

'THE MADDY!

BUCK'S GARBAGE SHIP!'

She caught my confused look, and waved her hand impatiently, gesturing for me to show her the diary. She made me flip back through the pages till I reached a set of blueprints.

'It's a spaceship to fly landfill into the sun,' she explained.

'Oh man, really?' said Ella Jane. 'That's what my mom's doing – building a spaceship?'

I heard an awkward little cough and looked round to find Tara had approached her daughter.

'Mom! If you'd just told me that, you could've saved yourself a whole lot of me whining about this place.'

Tara hugged her daughter. But she didn't look relieved, and I knew why.

'You're not, though, are you?' I said slowly. 'Not a ship that's ever going to make it to the sun.'

Got to love having an engineer on Team TARDIS!

I held up the blueprints. 'This is just a load of components chucked together. It looks like a kid drew it – no offence, Ella Jane. But what you're building is just an idea. It's a ship that wants to be able to reach orbit, not one that actually can. What I don't get is, I know that just from a quick look, and I haven't even got my NVQ. How did you not know?'

'She did,' said the Doctor quietly. 'They all did.'

Tara looked ashamed. 'I came on to the project a few months in. I could see right away that the others knew it was a joke, but I'd watched Greensville crumble to nothing when I was a kid. The *Maddy* project was bringing it all back. A new town, new jobs, a new home for so many families. It was wonderful. We all wanted it to last.'

'And you,' said the Doctor, shaking her head at Tomiko. 'Riding the solar winds in a neutrino-powered ship? Neutrinos pass straight through matter. They aren't going to power anything!'

'OK!' Tomiko threw up her hands. 'I heard you the first time. I'm not a space-travel expert. I just wanted to play around with the theory and Buck gave me my own neutrino detector. How could I say no to that?'

'So the whole plan's a bust?' asked Graham. 'The ship, the sun, all of it?'

The Doctor was smiling. 'Nope. It's a brilliant plan! Well, half of it is. The sun's a huge ball of energy that'll burn up anything. I don't recommend throwing a load of methane and hydrogen sulphide at it – you'll get toasted. But the basic idea's smart enough, if getting to the sun didn't use up more energy than it could ever save. Which means it might save us from this little – big – problem.'

She nodded up at massive Graham.

'The ship won't fly,' said Tara.

'That's what Katz tech is for!' said the Doctor. 'Not just fixing something that's broken. The animator virus takes an idea and brings it to life. If we feed it the plans, it'll chuck all its energy into constructing the ship. Then, we send it up into orbit, far away from any humans, skeletons or pumpkins, and right into the sun.'

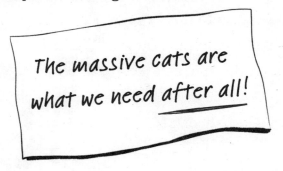

The massive cats are what we need after all!

The Doctor stopped holding giant Graham under control with the sonic. Instead, she used it to scan the blueprints from the diary and then sent them up to the giant, like she was uploading a file to a computer.

The giant lifted its great head, as if scenting something on the air like a dog. Then it began to run, homing in on two abandoned cars by the side of the road. Black beads flowed from the giant's hands over both cars, and they roared to life. Then, the giant climbed aboard as if the cars were two roller skates, and sped away over the horizon.

'Come on,' said Tomiko. 'There are monitors of the *Maddy*'s construction area at the Institute. We can watch it from there.'

A ride in Tara's car and a hairy lift trip later, we were in a boardroom deep underground.

I wiped off all my zombie make-up on my torn top. Ella Jane dumped her gorilla suit on her mum. We were both pretty over Halloween by then.

There's actually *a planet* called Halloween, I keep meaning to visit.

'That's Buck Green,' whispered Yaz, nodding at an old man in the corner with his head in his hands. 'Poor guy. I don't think he's taking all this too well.' The man looked like something inside him had broken.

To be honest, I was more worried about Graham. He wasn't making daft jokes. He wasn't trying to cheer us all along, or save the day. He wasn't even worrying about me. He just stood by himself watching the screens, while the Doctor and Tomiko pored over the big table, arguing in whispers about the plans.

'You OK, Graham?' I asked, joining him at the bank of monitors.

'I wish I knew,' he said. He looked down at his hands, turning them this way and that, and then stared at the image on the monitor. Giant Graham was in the warehouse on the other side of town, building a spaceship.

'Do you think a man can be bad without knowing it?' he asked.

I shrugged.

'That's the wrong question,' said Buck quietly. 'Every bad man is bad without knowing it. It's what he does when he realises he's bad. That's what matters.'

Buck looked up at the monitors. In one, the old town was still crowded with people trying to fathom what had happened. In another, the metal hull of the *Maddy* was swarming with the strange glossy beetle things.

Buck sighed deeply. 'Oh, who am I kidding? I've tried making amends. Maybe some things can't be forgiven.'

Graham looked even sadder.

'OI!' said the Doctor. 'I'm not having that, Buck Green. That big idea of yours – your magic neutrino-powered ship – that's never going to work, sorry. But trying out new ideas to help save this planet, bringing back hope to this town at the same time – that's worthwhile. That's good. You've done good. So the *Maddy* isn't going to be on the front page of every newspaper for saving the Earth from ecological disaster. That doesn't matter. Not everything has to be big news. The little things matter, too. You're building something here, for real people.'

She paused, looking at Tomiko, and at Ella Jane and Tara.

Tara stepped forward, nervously tucking a

stray hair behind her ear.

'I remember Maddy,' she said quietly. 'We weren't friends, but . . . I remember her. She's remembered. I remember the old town, too. That's why we stayed, Buck. Me, Tomiko, everyone working on the ship. You were building us a new home.'

Buck's lips pressed tightly together, like he was trying to hold in his feelings.

'Take that, Buck,' said the Doctor softly.

'Make the new town your daughter's legacy. It can be a hub for new scientific discoveries – an ecotown. Or even just a home. That'd be good, too. You could be proud of that.'

I didn't like being so far underground. I wanted to leave.

But Graham wouldn't, not till he'd seen it with his own eyes: his giant, still rebuilding and swarming over the now-completed hull of the spaceship.

The monitors showed us all angles as the warehouse cameras shifted view.

The engines fired. The spaceship took off. It soared into the darkening sky at incredible speed, until it disappeared out of sight. We followed its progress on one of the monitors. A tiny blip tracked by a red line.

WE WAITED.

Then, the red line stopped flashing. It faded to nothing. The old man blinked away tears. The *Maddy* had flown into the sun.

Giant Graham was gone for good.

I gave Ella Jane and her mum a little wave goodbye, then followed Yaz, Graham and the Doctor into the cool safety of the TARDIS.

As the doors closed, I checked the date in the diary.

DATELINE:
THURSDAY 31 OCTOBER, 2019
EARTH

Still 31 October. Still Halloween.

'So, all that was for nothing?' I asked. 'We're still stuck in time.'

The Doctor clapped me on the arm. 'Not for nothing, Ryan! Buck's learned a thing or two. Ella Jane and her mum got talking. Tomiko – ooh, I am dead cross with her – but she learned

something, too.' The Doctor got busy at the console, hands flying. Then a crinkle appeared above her nose.

'Not good news?' asked Yaz.

The Doctor was grim. 'No. Look – the time stasis is still in place. And it's growing.'

She waved a hand across the console. Golden lines floated in the air, flowing and moving like a linear replica of the swirly vortex that had tried to eat Yaz. It came to a rigid halt. Time was moving forward like it should, then it stopped dead.

'I think it's time we dealt with the question we're not asking,' said the Doctor, stepping back. 'Tomiko was in Texas, not Japan. That Katz ship just happened to be there, under the detector. The lake just happened to collapse, to show us the Katz ship was there, right on cue. Almost like it was meant to once we were there. As if something triggered it. Or someone.'

'About that,' said Graham quietly.

'It's a coincidence, innit?' I don't know why I said it so fast. I just knew a conversation was coming that I didn't want to have.

'Don't believe in coincidence,' said the Doctor. She looked at Graham. 'First I thought it was the TARDIS: a space–time anomaly all of its own. But that would've started things the instant we landed. I think something else triggered it, and I think one of us knows that.'

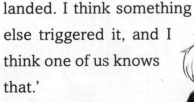

'Stop! Please, stop!'

Graham raised his hands, his voice cracking with exhaustion. I couldn't remember ever seeing him so upset; not since Nan.

'It was me, OK? I don't know what I did, or how I did it. But it was me. I set that lake off. Yaz, you saw it, too. Don't pretend you didn't. It went funny the second I stepped near it. Ryan, son, I'm sorry. I don't know what's the matter with me. Maybe I caught something from time travelling . . . space evil? Curse of the time traveller? Martian flu? Leave me behind if you have to. I don't want to hurt you – any of you.'

I was scared, then, really scared. She's brilliant, the Doctor. She's always on our side. But right then, at that second, she looked at Graham like he was someone she didn't know. Someone she wasn't sure she could trust.

The Doctor held out the sonic, her face still and steady as she scanned him.

She checked the read-out agonisingly slowly.

Then she smiled. 'You're just you, Graham. No space evil (which is not a thing, by the way). No curse. You're fine.'

He staggered, steadying himself on the edge of the console.

'Course, that leaves us still wondering what the trigger was,' the Doctor said.

She scanned Yaz.

Then she began to scan me.

'Hey!' I put my hands across my chest, feeling a little bit offended. 'I haven't got space evil!'

She frowned harder, stepping closer and scanning me again, head to toe.

'I wasn't even there for most of it!' I protested, panicking.

'Of course!' Her face broke into a huge smile of relief as she pointed at my pocket. 'The diary. A psychic diary is a power source like no other. If there's a disruption in the space–time continuum, this diary wouldn't show up as a tiny little blip. It's like a loudhailer, announcing our presence across the universe.'

'Announcing it to who?' asked Yaz.

The Doctor tilted her head. 'Now there's a question.'

BBC

DOCTOR WHO

Team TARDIS Diaries

PAPER MOON

Louie Stowell

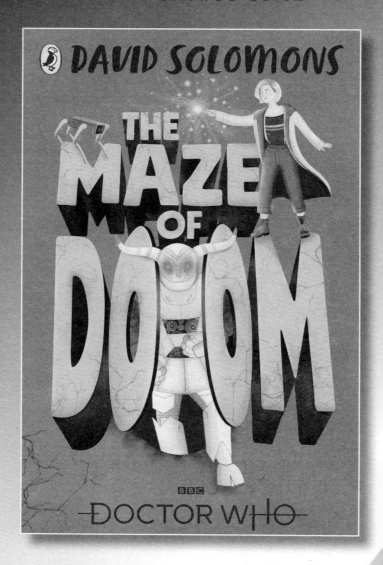

3. Nimon of Athens

London, United Kingdom, circa 2028 AD

'Where are we?' asked Yaz. 'Looks posh.'

'Palace of Whitehall,' said the Doctor. 'At least the only part of it still standing in your era. Last time I was here, they'd just beheaded Charles the First – right about there.' She indicated the spot on the pavement that Graham occupied. He swallowed and took a step to one side. The Doctor breezed past, heading for the building's entrance. 'Whatever overloaded our battery, we are seconds away from discovering it.'

They made it as far as the entrance hall before her prediction proved to be over-optimistic, their path barred by a pair of unsmiling security guards bulging out of tight-fitting suit jackets. Past the men, at the end of an arched corridor lit by candelabra, lay a set of double doors, and beyond those the source of the mysterious power signal. But for now the answer was tantalisingly out of reach.

'May I see your invitation?' asked the first guard. It was a toss-up as to which was shinier: his shoes or his bald head.

Graham knew that of course they had no invitation, but that never stopped the Doctor. Like a close-up magician at the climax of a trick, she opened her hand with a flourish and there on her palm lay what looked like a plain plastic wallet. Flipping it open to reveal a seemingly blank pad of white paper, she held it in front of the man's suspicious eyes.

The two guards squinted at the paper, their expressions slowly altering from wariness to acceptance. Graham had seen this happen – a lot. The wallet contained psychic paper, a Time Lord invention that showed whatever the holder wanted the viewer to see. Usually. Some people and alien races had the power to see through the deception, but it was clear to Graham that the guards were no match. As far as their brains were telling them, they were looking at an official invitation.

'This lot are my plus-three,' said the Doctor, thumbing over her shoulder at the others.

'You still can't come in,' snapped the bald guard.

'Why not?' said the Doctor, already angling to go past him.

He turned the blank pad round. 'See what it says right here?'

'Uhh . . .'

'Black tie,' added the guard helpfully. He cast a disapproving glance at the group, ending on Ryan's feet. 'And he's wearing trainers.'

Graham could tell that the Doctor was weighing up her options. Either she could attempt to argue her way past these guys or –

'We'll be right back,' she said and, spinning on her heel, led the others quickly back out on to the pavement and into the TARDIS.

As well as swimming pools, ballrooms and all the rest, the ship contained a voluminous walk-in wardrobe. It was more like a costume department, thought Graham as he searched racks of era-appropriate suits. *Moss Bros in the cosmos*. He squeezed into a traditional black tuxedo and went to look for a mirror. He found Ryan hogging one, admiring his own choice of outfit. The young man had picked a dinner suit in a deep shade of purple.

'You look like an aubergine,' said Graham.

Ryan gave a tug at his sleeves. 'I am rocking this suit.' He was used to his granddad's ribbing, but right now nothing could burst his bubble. He hadn't felt this good in ages. He wasn't sure what had caused the uplift, and he didn't question it too closely. All he knew was that he was buzzing. He adjusted his bow tie in the mirror. There was a gleam in his eye.

He peered closer at his reflection. Yes, there it was. An actual gleam in his left eye. Maybe a fragment of that exploding stone battery thing had got in there? But, if so, why wasn't it bothering him? A piece of grit like that would be irritating, if not downright painful, but he felt better than ever.

Before he could wonder any more about it, on the other side of the room the curtain of a dressing cubicle swept back and the Doctor and Yaz emerged in each other's arms. It took Ryan a moment to realise that they were dancing. The Doctor was leading. She was wearing a jumpsuit in a striking rust colour.

'Nice togs,' said Ryan admiringly.

'I love getting dressed up for a mission,' the Doctor said. 'It's by one of my favourite Zygon designers. No fiddly buttons, but the suckers do leave a mark.'

Yaz was in a long silver dress with a pattern like ripples on a moonlit pond.

'Ready?' asked the Doctor.

'Dip me,' replied Yaz.

The dancers came out of a turn, the Doctor twirled Yaz, then pulled her close, wrapped one hand firmly round her waist, cradled her neck with the other and gently lowered her to the floor as Yaz hugged the Doctor's shoulder.

There was a long silence as they stayed like that for several seconds.

'We should probably go now,' said Yaz.

'Yeah,' agreed the Doctor.

Second time round, they swept past the security guards and made their way swiftly along the candelabra-lit corridor, through the double doors and into what was a striking main hall. Graham took in the white fluted pillars that lined both sides of the soaring space, supporting a gallery that ran the whole way round the room, under a ceiling frescoed with fat babies and blokes in floaty robes. The glow from four low-hanging chandeliers reflected gold flecks in the ceiling and on the tops of the pillars, and shed warm light on the well-heeled guests who occupied the dozens of white-clothed round tables that reached across the polished floor like stepping stones.

'It's a double-cube,' said the Doctor. 'All the room's proportions are mathematically related to create a harmonious whole. The order is pleasing to the human mind, but it'll drive a Yeti nuts.'

'Noted,' said Graham. 'In the event of a Yeti invasion, seek out the nearest state ballroom.'

At the far end of the double-cube room, behind a podium on a raised stage, stood a thin man with a wave of shining golden hair. He looked like a struck match. Raising a small hammer in one hand, he lowered his mouth to a microphone.

'Sold!' he said, slamming down the hammer. It cracked against the podium like a gunshot.

Graham jumped.

The man gestured to an easel standing next to him on the stage, upon which sat an oil painting in an ornate frame. He turned to the audience and his golden wave of hair moved to point like a finger. 'Sold to the handsome industrialist in the good half of the Rich List.'

The man in question accepted the hooting congratulations of the other guests at his table.

Graham noticed that he was holding a small paddle with the number three on it. Evidently, they had arrived at some sort of auction. As an assistant wheeled the painting offstage, four more manhandled the next item on.

'And now we come to our final lot. Certainly the most unusual item to feature tonight. You'd better have a big entrance hall for this one – but of course you do.'

A tinkle of knowing laughter rose from the audience.

The item was shrouded beneath a white sheet but, judging from its outline, the object was roughly person-shaped, though taller and wider.

The Doctor produced her second alien device of the evening, a gently curved silver talon that sat snugly across her palm. Its mostly metal body was interlaced with a lava-coloured mineral and set with a single crystal at one end, which glowed when the device was in use. She called it her sonic screwdriver. Graham had been present when she constructed the device, a potent combination of Sheffield steel and Gallifreyan tech. Wielded by the Doctor, it could analyse almost any substance, open almost any door, assemble almost any bookcase. She aimed it across the room at the object. A second later, the sonic chirped and the Doctor studied its findings on a narrow display.

'That's what we came for. The same technology that blew up on the TARDIS is under that sheet.'

At that moment the auctioneer tugged at the sheet and it floated to the floor. There was a gasp from the audience as the object was revealed.

'It's a giant Oscar statue,' said Ryan.

'That's no Oscar,' said Yaz. 'It's a whatchamacallit. Y'know, story about that bull-thing killed by the guy who goes into the maze with the thread so he can find his way out again.'

'Minotaur,' said Graham.

The statue was the colour of molten bronze, its hulking body that of a muscle-bound man, but with the bluff head of a bull, from which sprung horns like handlebars.

'Looks like a Nimon to me,' said the Doctor.

Yaz had come to recognise the Doctor's differing tones of voice. There was regular concern followed by deep unease, and then a level of fear that caused her to make light-hearted jokes. Thankfully, she didn't seem to be at the most extreme level. Yet.

'An alien race, possibly the origin of your Minotaur myth. Romana and I came across them once.'

'I thought the Minotaur was Greek, not Roman,' said Graham.

'*Romana,*' the Doctor repeated, her gaze drifting off. 'Old friend.' She brightened. 'My canine companion was with us back then. Like your cop show, Yaz.'

Yaz blushed, as Ryan and Graham exchanged baffled looks.

'A rare example of what is believed to be a Minoan temple guard,' declared the auctioneer. 'Recently recovered from the depths of the Aegean Sea, and in quite remarkable condition. One of only two in the world, the other held in the private collection of Panos and Penelope Polichroniadis. Who will start me at half a million pounds?'

There was a momentary hush of expectation, and then at the table directly in front of the auctioneer a hand went up holding a small paddle sporting the number one.

Half a million! Graham looked around the room, wondering who could be foolish enough to outbid that kind of money.

'One million pounds!' sang out the Doctor.